T0197612

Bibia Meets Gripper

By Purnima Mead

Illustrated By Kathy Kerber

WestBow Press books may be ordered through booksellers or by contacting:

WestBow Press
A Division of Thomas Nelson & Zondervan
1663 Liberty Drive
Bloomington, IN 47403
www.westbowpress.com
844-714-3454

ISBN: 978-1-4497-9751-5 (sc)

Library of Congress Control Number: 2013910258

Print information available on the last page.

WestBow Press rev. date: 09/01/2023

Dedication

To Penelope Hope Marie Mead, Rehan Alejandro Singh, Dastaan Emilio Singh, never stop dreaming cause if you can dream it, you can make it happen.

This Book Belongs To:

_____

Fall had set in! The colors of the leaves were not green any more! They were green once! But now they are orange, yellow, red and crimson. It looked as if the forest was on fire, but it was the bright colors of the season. When the leaves change its color, it is Fall! Fall has another name, and it is called 'Autumn'. Bibia knew she would meet her forest friends once again; she has a smile on her face each time she thinks about her forest friends.

3

"I jump up high; I jump down low, over the mountains and the valleys below; not too fast yet not too slow". Bibia turned around to see who it was; she heard it again, and this time it was louder, "I jump up high; I jump down low, over the mountains and the valleys below; not too fast yet, not too slow" Who can this be? Bibia wondered; "Who is it? Who is there?" Bibia called out.

"It is me Bibia! I am here; turn around". Bibia turned around and saw, there was *somebody* hiding behind a tree. Bibia could only see the face; and rest of the body was hidden. "Who are you"? Asked Bibia. "I am your friend and I jump up high; I jump down low, over the mountains and valleys below; Not too fast yet not too slow", said *somebody* from behind the tree, with a low voice. "I have not seen you before and you are not my friend, my friends are in the forest and I know all of their names," said Bibia

"I am Gripper! Gripper The Grasshopper!" Gripper said, with a smiling face. Gripper was a very friendly grasshopper; he loved to make new friends. He was funny, crazy and silly all in a sweet way. Gripper made everyone laugh with his silly jokes, everyone liked him and wanted him to be around them - but no one knew from where Gripper had come. Gripper appeared and disappeared...! No one would know from where he came and where he's gone. Gripper was like a MYSTERY!! Somewhat! He even knew Bibia by her name ah!

"Gripper The Grasshopper? And why is he so green? Why does Gripper not have colors like me?" Bibia wondered. Bibia wanted to meet Mr. Rainbow so she could tell him to share his colors with Gripper; if only Mr. Rainbow could share his colors with Gripper then Gripper too will have orange, red, pink, yellow, purple, blue and green... oh no not green, Gripper was green already and Bibia thought that green would not be a good idea.

"What are you thinking about Bibia?" asked Gripper. "I am thinking of calling Mr. Rainbow" answered Bibia. "Mr. Rainbow? Who is he?" asked Gripper. "Mr. Rainbow has a lot of colors and I am sure he will be willing to share some colors with you, look at you, you are all green, and only green," said Bibia. "This is because I am different from you, and we all are different from each other", said Gipper - and I can jump up high, jump down low, over the mountains and valleys below, not too fast, yet not too slow. "Do you know Bibia, that I can leap up to 20 times my length?" said Gripper. "No I did not know, I only know that you are green and you can hop," answered Bibia. "And I am a grasshopper," said Gripper with a smile on his face.

"Ah I can see my forest friends, there they are," Bibia told Gripper, pointing at her forest friends. "There is Mr. Bouncy, Mr. Squeaky, and Miss Rollie," said Bibia. "Are they green too," asked Gripper, with funny a smile on his face. "No', said Bibia while laughing with Gripper.

Bibia's forest friends were coming towards Bibia and Gripper; and they all had a smile on their face, they knew that they were going to make a new friend today - one more friend. "Can I be your friend too?' asked Gripper. "Yes, you can be my friend and our friend too," said Bibia.

"Hi friends, meet Gripper , Gripper The Grasshopper," said Bibia. "Hello," said Gripper to all the friends. Bibia knew that she was going to have a good time with her forest friends and with a new friend, Gripper - Bibia was missing Mr. Simley The Sun and Mr. Rainbow.

"Come let us sit and talk, I can smell the ripe pumpkins and the fresh smell of Fall", said Bibia. The forest friends all took a deep breath, and they could smell the fresh and ripe pumpkins around too. They also loved the smell of the pumpkin pie with all kinds of yummy spices. To have lots of friends, and to have new friends seemed like a wonderful feeling of friendship for everyone in the forest.

17

Bibia and the forest friends sat around Gripper.

"I have one more thing to tell you about me," said Gripper. "What, What is it?" everyone looked at Gripper and asked. "I can not only leap 20 times my length, I can also see forwards, backwards and sideways and I have 3 eyes," Gripper said. "So you can see what is happening behind you now?" asked Bibia. "No, only when there is a predator I suppose, you all are my friends, and I don't have to fear anything", said Gripper. "Three eyes? I wish I had three eyes" said Miss Rollie. "I am an insect too, just like Bibia is, and I have 10,000 kinds of species like me all over the world - and I have green blood in me," said Gripper.

"And I don't have ears," said Gripper. "Oh we can hear you, but you cannot hear us, so it means you can't hear what we are saying?" said Bibia. "I said, I don't have ears but that does not mean I can't hear you. I can sense sound with an organ in my body, which is called *tympanum* ⟨tim-pan-um⟩" said Gripper. Gripper The Grasshopper was enjoying telling about himself to his new friends. He knew that he was not like the forest friends or like Bibia The Butterfly at all, and that was what made him different and so special.

The forest friends and Bibia were happy to have Gripper as their new friend - each one of them was different from the other and that is how they knew that they were all so special.

They went their ways, with a nice feeling in their heart, a feeling of being special and different, and thankful for good friends.

⟨Note: Haemolymph circulates nutrients through the body and carries metabolic wastes to the melphighian tubes to be excreted, because it does not carry oxygen, grasshopper's blood is green.⟩

Printed in the United States
by Baker & Taylor Publisher Services